Based on a translation by Susan Beard

First published in Swedish as
Lilla syster Kanin går alldeles vilse
by Bonnier Carlsen Bokförlag
Text © 1987 Ulf Nilsson
Illustrations © 1987 Eva Eriksson
English version © 2017 Floris Books
All rights reserved. No part of this publication may be reproduced
without the prior permission of Floris Books, Edinburgh
www.florisbooks.co.uk
British Library CIP Data available
ISBN 978-178250-377-4
Printed in Malaysia

Little Sister Rabbit Gets Lost

Ulf Nilsson and Eva Eriksson

Floris Books

Little Sister Rabbit lived in a burrow with Mother Rabbit, Father Rabbit and Big Brother Rabbit. But today she was going out on an adventure all by herself. She waved goodbye to her big brother.

She hopped and stamped in all the puddles.
Splash!

Her shoes got soaking wet.

She plopped pebbles down a drain. This was her favourite game. She played it for two whole hours as the sun rose higher in the sky and the birds sang happily.

Plop. Plop. Plop. Plop. Plop.

She pretended to be a scary ghost.
Boo!
And tried to frighten every tiny bug she met.
But they weren't really afraid …

Soon Little Sister Rabbit came to the river, which flowed along like a lazy old eel.

She built rickety little boats to sail out of leaves and twigs – her own extra special kind of boats.

She was glad Big Brother Rabbit wasn't there to tell her what boats should really look like.

Next she came to the lake, which was flat and shiny, like a big silver coin.

Little Sister Rabbit skimmed stones and watched them bounce a long way.

One ... two ... three ... plop! Three bounces!

She was glad Big Brother Rabbit wasn't there to show her how to throw them even further.

Then she turned cartwheels faster and
faster... When she stopped she was so
dizzy that she didn't know where she was.

Suddenly she realised she was lost. Oh no!
How would she get back to her burrow?

She peered under a tree.
Was this the right burrow?

No, some other rabbits lived here, with long serious noses.
She knew it wasn't polite to laugh at other people's noses.
Little Sister Rabbit left quickly.

She hopped on through the wood and found
another door. Was this the right house?

No, this was Mr Badger's home, an old and very grand gentleman.
He didn't like to be disturbed.
Little Sister Rabbit left quickly.

She looked under a root.
Was this the right place?

Little Sister Rabbit tiptoed into the dark
tunnel. Inside there was a strange smell.
She heard snoring. Was this her burrow?

No, it was a foxes' den! They were asleep,
growling in their dreams.
Little Sister Rabbit left *very* quickly.

Little Sister Rabbit ran away from the foxes' den as fast as her wobbly legs could carry her.

She felt very scared. She started to cry. And it was beginning to rain.

But then she heard someone calling, "Little Sister Rabbit!
Where are you?"

And there was her brave Big Brother
Rabbit. He reached for her paw, and told her,
in a gentle and comforting kind of way, that
she must be more careful.

Together they hopped along, all the way
back home.